Dedications

Author: "For all children: each one special and unique.
They are truly the best part of this world."

Illustrator: "For Jeff, my baseball mentor and best
friend. May God favor us with extra innings."

The Pickle Man: Dreaming of the Majors

Published by Strategic Book Publishing
An Imprint of Writers Literary & Publishing Services, Inc.
845 Third Avenue, Sixth Floor - 6016
New York, New York 10022

ISBN: 978-1-934925-72-0 / SKU: 1-934925-72-1

The Pickle Man:

Dreaming of the Majors

Written by Susan Seeber Holloran

Illustrations by Laurie Wood Halvorson

This summer on July 11th,
I turned eight years old,
but I've been playing
on a baseball team
since I was five.

6

My big brother, Josh,
taught me how to
hold the bat and swing,
way back when I was only three.

7

Josh is the best brother any kid could have, and he's awesome at bat! Seven times out of ten, Josh hits one over the fence for his team, the Baseline Braves.
He spends a lot of time in batting practice, and we play catch In our backyard every chance we get.

9

Josh says we're the luckiest kids on the block because our
house backs up to the school park. When there isn't a
game going on, we peel out through our back gate toward
the worn-down dirt mound.

Josh pitches to me
and I run the bases.

11

I almost always hit a double or triple for my team, the Centennial Brewers. Coach Gray says I've got great speed.

"You're like a steam locomotive out there, kid!"

My mom tosses her head back when I hit a good one and yelps, "Atta'way, Za-man! What a hit! Now fly!" Mom always says, "Fly."

She told me once that when I run, my feet go so fast she thinks they'll leave the ground.

Mom says that watching me and Josh play baseball is her favorite thing to do. She cheers really loud, so she must like it a lot!

17

My grandpa can't see very well. He says that's what happens when your eyes get old, but he still comes to all my games. He can tell which one is me because of my white-blond hair.

"You're a real towhead, Zacho, just like your mom."
Grandpa chuckles when he talks.

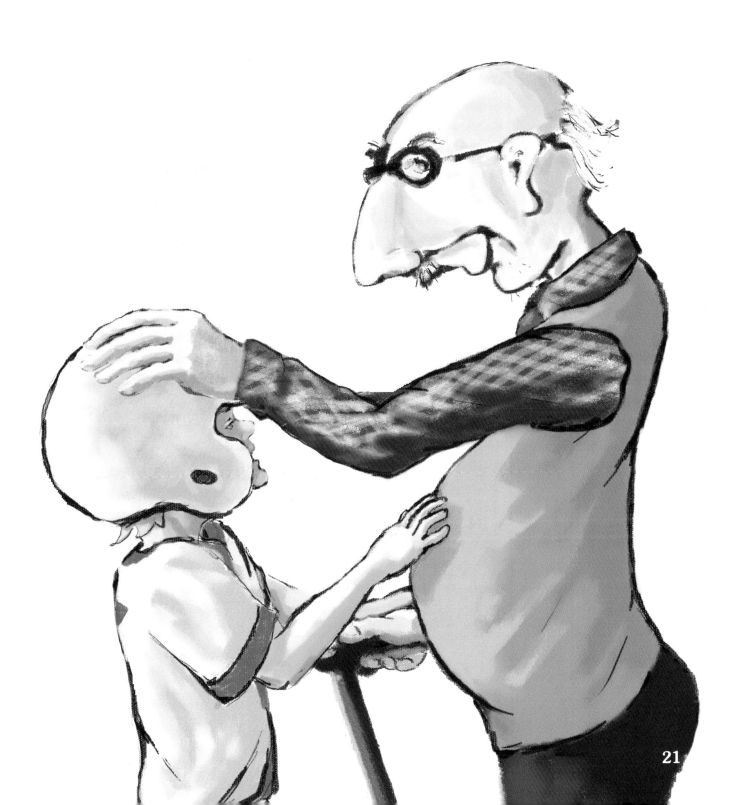

My dad says I'm a smart player, and that I think fast on my feet. He always hollers, "Way to read the play, Zach. That's the way to get a jump on it!"

I'm real stubborn, like my dad. That's probably why I'm always getting into pickles.

22

I like getting stuck between the bases
while the other team tries to tag me out.
It's fun to dodge them with my fast moves!

My coach is right about me being fast, but Josh is the power hitter. When I'm big like Josh I'll hit one right over the fence.

I'll trot around the bases with my arms straight up in the air, and I'll take my time doing it, just like the pros.

I watched Josh hit a home run against the Apache Socks.

When he rounded the bases, that's what he did -- arms straight up.

Josh and I like to imagine hitting homers when we play in the park. We make crowd noises and pretend the game is sold out.

I bet someday Josh will pitch for the pros, maybe for the Rockies. He'll pitch a no hitter and I'll be there to see it.

When I play in the pros,
they'll call me the pickle man,
and the speaker will crackle
with the voice of the play-by-
play man as he announces:

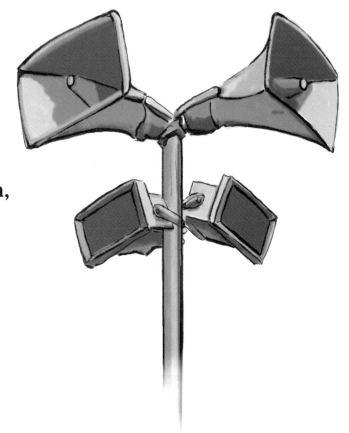

"Welcome to Fenway Park, ladies and gentlemen.
It's a scorcher day here in Boston, and strolling up
to the plate is Zach the pickle man, as he's known
to his teammates."

"This guy packs a powerful pickle!"

30

"Hee-ere's the pitch!
It's a curve ball low and outside.

Zach lets it go by.
Ball one."

31

"Now the pitcher delivers a fastball high and inside.
Zach swings and fouls it back.
That makes the count one and one.
No problem for the pickle man, folks.
He looks cool as a cucumber out there."

33

"The pitcher blows another fastball right over the plate. Zach hits! It's a line drive up the alley for an easy double."

"Wait just a minute!"

"He's rounded second
and is heading for third --
Oh my!"

"There's the throw to third base. Is he out?"

"Nooo!"

"The ball is thrown behind him as he darts back
toward second and slides head first into the base!"

"I can barely see the
signal through his dust."

"Is he safe?"

"This sold-out crowd is on their feet. What a grand and gutsy play by the pickle man. He pulls it out again!"

This summer when I played for the Brewers, I got into seven pickles.

I was never tagged once.

Some of my friends say that to get into the pros you've got to have "an edge." I think that means you've got to have something special going for you; something that makes you different from everyone else.

My mom and my coach think that being fast is my edge. My dad thinks that playing smart, and being fast, is my edge.

I think Josh is my edge. He was always around to play ball with me long before I became the pickle man. He is my brother, and my teacher, and my best friend. He's probably pitched to me more than two thousand times.

Someday Josh and I will play together in the pros.

He'll pitch from the hill and I'll round the bases.

1 John 3: 18-19: My dear children, let's not just talk about love; let's practice real love. This is the only way we'll know we're living truly, living in God's reality.

(The Message//Remix)

Susan Seeber Holloran has acted professionally on stage, in television, and in radio. She's taught pre-kindergarten through third grade, and has written and directed children's plays and musical productions. Her love for writing evolved through her many years of story telling in the theater. Susan enjoys running, biking, and hiking with her husband Tom, and cherishes time spent with family. She is the mother of two terrific young men and one beautiful daughter-in-law. Her sons are the inspiration for this book.

Susan Holloran

Laurie Wood Halvorson was born in Colorado and raised in western Nebraska. She attended Rocky Mountain School of Art and Doane College. Laurie has been blessed with a loving husband, three amazing children, and to date, one delightful grandson. Her favorite pastimes include painting, motorbikes and spending time with friends. Laurie credits God's mercy for bringing her from depression into new life and restoring her creative gifts.

Printed in the United States
145010LV00002B

9 781934 925720